HOME GROUND

HOME GROUND

ALAN GIBBONS

With illustrations by
Chris Chalik

Barrington Stoke

First published in 2019 in Great Britain by
Barrington Stoke Ltd
18 Walker Street, Edinburgh, EH3 7LP

www.barringtonstoke.co.uk

Text © 2019 Alan Gibbons
Illustrations © 2019 Chris Chalik

A CIP catalogue record for this book is available
from the British Library upon request

ISBN: 978-1-78112-856-5

Printed in China by Leo

Contents

Chapter 1
Hasan

He was there again – the boy Sam had seen
before. He was standing by the fence. Sam had
seen him every week at the sports centre. He
came with some older boys and played on the
next pitch. He was fast and skilful. Because he
was younger and smaller than the rest of his
team, he got knocked over a lot, but he always
picked himself up. Sam didn't know why he
played in a team with kids that were older than
him. One thing stuck out. It was the boy's hair.
It made him look a bit like Mo Salah.

Suddenly, Sam heard a shout to his left.

"Wake up!" Jordan yelled.

It was too late. The striker Sam was meant to mark was powering past him, and Sam was on the back foot. Sam tried to get back, but he was too late. He swung a leg to cut off the attack, but he couldn't get in a tackle. The striker left Sam behind, ran wide and crossed the ball, leaving the keeper in no man's land. Another player was waiting in the goalmouth.

He tapped the ball into the empty net. "Goal!" shouted the players on the other team.

Sam's team captain, Jordan, was really angry. His face was hard. His eyes were popping.

"What's wrong with you?" he yelled, and came right up close to Sam. "You're not here to day-dream. You're here to defend."

Sam felt sick – he'd given a goal away. His team, West Park Celtic, was second from bottom in the league and the boys couldn't afford another defeat. There were two divisions in their league and they didn't want to get relegated.

Jordan was still yelling. His eyes were hard like stones.

"All you need is a big red nose and floppy shoes," Jordan shouted, "and you'd be the biggest clown on the pitch."

Sam could feel his eyes sting. But he wasn't going to show he was upset. "I didn't do it on purpose," he said. "I switched off for a moment, that's all."

"Yes," Jordan snapped, "and that's all it takes. Your day-dreaming cost us a goal." He shoved Sam in the chest. "You're useless."

Jordan shook his head and stomped off.

Sam didn't want to look at his team-mates. It was so unfair. He knew he'd been one of Celtic's best players over the season. Jordan was a big mouth. He was always shouting for the ball, but he wasn't half as good as he thought he was. He lost possession most of the time and wasted chances. He always took the free kicks and penalties, but he missed them way too often. *How does he get away with it?* Sam thought.

Jordan planted the ball on the centre spot and clapped his hands.

"We're only one goal down," he told the rest of the team. "Concentrate."

Sam knew what was coming next. Jordan turned to Sam and tapped his own forehead. "That means you, idiot."

That was too much for Jack Rigby, their manager.

"Knock it off, Jordan," he shouted. "Show the other boys some respect. You're not helping."

Jordan scowled. He didn't like getting told off.

*

Celtic played better for the rest of the half, but they were still 2–1 down and heading for their third defeat in a row.

"Well, at least you didn't give another goal away," Jordan said softly, so that Jack couldn't hear.

That made Sam angry.

"Say that again and I'll thump you," he warned. "We should stick up for each other. You missed a pen last week and I didn't say a word about it."

Jordan didn't like Sam talking about his missed penalty.

"That's because you wouldn't dare," Jordan sneered. "You're a coward."

Sam shoved Jordan in the chest. Then Jordan pushed him back. They had hold of each other's shirts, ready to fight.

"Stop right there!" Jack said, and stood between them. "Who started this?"

Jordan pointed at Sam.

"He did. He attacked me for nothing. He's off his head," Jordan said.

"Did anyone else see what happened?" Jack asked.

Another boy, Kai, stepped up.

"Sam started it," Kai said.

"OK, Sam," Jack said. "I'm subbing you."

Sam couldn't believe it.

"That's not fair," he shouted. "Jordan was winding me up."

"Then you need to get better at taking the banter," Jack said. "You're always going to get insults. It's part of being a footballer."

Sam dropped onto the grass and watched the rest of the team jog back onto the pitch. That's when he remembered the boy by the fence. Sam turned round to see if he was still there. The boy was in goal now, but he saw Sam looking. When his game finished, the boy came over to talk.

"The manager was wrong to take you off," he said to Sam. "You didn't start the fight." He pointed at Jordan. "He did."

Sam nodded. "I know. Jordan's crafty like that. You're not from round here, are you?"

"I am," the boy said. "I live in the flats over there."

"You know what I mean," Sam said. "That isn't a Liverpool accent."

The boy grinned. "I'm from Iraq," he said. "I came here with my family. We're refugees."

He waved his hand in the direction of the team on the next pitch. "My whole team is refugees. See those guys?" He pointed out two men standing by the goal. "They are from a local football club. They raised money for our kit and boots."

"Nice one," Sam said. "So what's your name?"

"I'm Hasan." He put out his hand and Sam shook it.

"You're lucky to be in a team with boys the same age as you," Hasan said. "Everybody in my team is older. They don't give me the ball and they make me play in goal – even my brother." He pointed to the tallest player on the team. "I wish I was in a team like yours."

Sam didn't feel very lucky to be playing for West Park Celtic. They got beaten more often than an egg.

"We're second from bottom," Sam said. "We're rubbish."

"So get some new players," Hasan said.

That gave Sam an idea.

"Do you want to play for us?" he said. "I can talk to Jack. We play five-a-side here every Wednesday to train."

"That sounds good," Hasan said.

Just then they heard a lot of shouts and groans. Celtic had given another goal away.

"That's done it," Sam said. "We're going to be bottom of the league after this result."

Hasan laughed. "Then you definitely need me."

WHAT IS A REFUGEE?

Refugees are ordinary people like you and me. They have to leave their home country because they are in danger. This could be because of war or a natural disaster. Or they could be at risk of being badly treated by their own government.

There are about 60 million people in the world who have had to flee their homes. Many of them live in camps. Refugee camps are not good places to live. People often have to sleep in tents or even steel containers that are hot and stuffy.

The biggest refugee camp in the world is currently in Kutupalong in Bangladesh. Turkey is home to more refugees than any other country – over 3 million. Less than 1 per cent of the world's refugees come to the UK.

Many refugees make long, dangerous journeys to escape war and fighting in their own countries. Some pay to get on a boat to cross the sea, but many of the boats are leaky and not good enough for the crossing. Thousands of refugees have drowned on their journeys.

Other people get on lorries or trains. Often they have to hide. It can be very dangerous, and some have been hurt or killed. Sometimes there is no food or water. People have even suffocated because there was no air in the back of the lorry.

When refugees do manage to reach another country safely, they aren't always welcome. When they are waiting to see if a new country will take them in, they are called asylum seekers.

Chapter 2
"He doesn't talk"

It rained a lot that next Wednesday, so Sam thought maybe Hasan wouldn't turn up for the five-a-side training. But he was there before anybody else, waiting by the goal. The rain was running down his face. There was another boy with him.

"This is Faisal," Hasan said. "He doesn't talk."

Sam stared at Faisal. His face was like a mask. "He's got to say something."

Hasan gave a shrug. "He doesn't say much to me. He never talks to strangers. He has seen too many bad things."

What does Hasan mean? Sam thought, but he didn't ask. It might be rude.

Soon, the other boys started to turn up. Jack Rigby arrived in his car. "Where's John?" he asked, looking around.

"He's dropped out," Jordan said. "He's fed up of losing. We all are."

Jack frowned.

"That isn't a very good attitude," he said. "You can't win every match."

"We don't win any of them," Jordan said. "We've only won twice all season."

"So what have we got to do, boys?" Jack said. He tried to sound cheerful.

"Try harder?" was one answer.

"Cheat," another boy said, and everybody laughed.

"You've got to work for each other," Jack said. "You've got to play as a team."

He looked over at Hasan and Faisal.

"I see we've got two new players. Come over here, lads. I'll have to get you registered."

He wrote down the boys' details. "I'll have to talk to your parents," Jack said.

"Faisal doesn't have any," Hasan said.

"What do you mean, 'doesn't have any'?" Jordan wanted to know. "Who does he live with?"

"He lives with his foster parents," Hasan explained.

"How did he get here then?" Jordan asked.

"Lorries," Hasan answered, "and a boat."

Jordan laughed. "Are you trying to be funny?" he asked.

Hasan shook his head and stared back as if Jordan was trying to play a trick on him. "You wanted to know," he said, "so I told you."

Jordan was getting angry now. He didn't like the new boys.

Jack split the boys into two teams and blew the whistle to start the game. "We've got too many for five-a-side," he said. "One or two of you will have to sit out. I will take boys off from time to time and bring others on to replace them. That way, you will all get a turn."

Sam got the ball from the kick-off and rolled it to Hasan. He was facing Jordan. He poked the ball between Jordan's feet and ran round him, slotting the ball into the net.

1–0.

"You got nutmegged," Sam shouted as he jogged past Jordan.

Hasan made Jordan look stupid again two minutes later. This time he rolled the ball forward as if he was asking Jordan to tackle him, then he dragged it back and went past him. He crossed the ball and another boy poked it home. Jordan fell over and landed on his backside. He wasn't just fed up. He was angry because he was being made to look stupid.

When Hasan got the ball a third time, Jordan didn't wait. He pushed towards Hasan and ran his foot down his shin. Hasan rolled over on the ground. It hurt!

"That was out of order," Jack said. "Get off the pitch, Jordan. I'll have a word with you later."

Hasan got to his feet, but he was limping badly.

"You have a bit of a rest, son," Jack said. "Let's see what your mate can do."

Hasan was good, but Faisal was amazing. He was taller and stronger than Hasan. He didn't do as many tricks, but he had such close control, nobody could get the ball off him. He scored twice with his feet and once with his head.

"OK, Faisal," Jack said. "Take a rest. Are you ready to come back on, Hasan?"

Hasan nodded and showed more of his tricks. He did two step-overs, then rolled the ball into the net.

As they walked off the pitch, Sam nudged Hasan. "Keep an eye on Jordan," he said. "He doesn't like anybody making a fool of him. Let Faisal know too."

Hasan grinned. "You can tell Faisal yourself," he said. "He isn't stupid, you know. He understands everything you say. He just doesn't say anything back."

Sam thought about Faisal. Hasan said he had seen too many bad things. What did that mean?

The boys stood round Jack. "OK, lads," he said. "John has dropped out, but it looks as if we have struck lucky. We've got a couple of good players to take his place. I'm playing both of them on Sunday."

"Are you having a laugh?" Jordan asked. "They can't just walk into the team."

"Who's the manager, Jordan?" Jack said. "Me or you?"

Jordan waited for a few moments. "You," he said.

"That's right," Jack said, "and don't forget it. We haven't won for four games. We defend all right, but we're not scoring enough goals."

Jordan glared. "Are you blaming me?" he asked.

"No," Jack said, "I'm not blaming anyone. But we need more pace. Hasan and Faisal have got bucket loads. I'm playing Hasan in the centre of midfield. Faisal will be upfront alongside you, Jordan."

Jordan turned bright red. He looked as if his head was going to explode. "I don't need anybody alongside me. I just need somebody to give me the ball. You can't score goals without the right kind of service."

Jack waited for him to finish. "You'll do as you're told, Jordan," he said. "You can't do everything on your own, so you need support. Now you've got it. We'll see how you can get on with Faisul."

Sam read the look on Jordan's face. He didn't think Faisal and Jordan would ever be friends.

CHILD REFUGEES

Many refugees are young people who have lost their families. They are often very lonely and afraid when they arrive in a strange new country where they don't know anyone or speak the language.

Over 80 years ago, nearly 4,000 children came to the UK to escape from the Spanish Civil War. Not everyone wanted the children to come to Britain, but they arrived in Southampton in May 1937.

They were taken to a campsite where they lived in tents for a few months. The British government did not pay for food for the children, but ordinary people gave money to help them.

When the Spanish Civil War was over, many of the children went back to their families in Spain, but some stayed in the UK. Some fought for the British Army in the Second World War, and six of them became professional footballers and played for teams in the English League. One of those was Emilio Aldecoa, who played for Wolverhampton Wanderers and Coventry City.

Another famous group of child refugees arrived in Britain at the beginning of the Second World War. They came to Britain as part of the Kindertransport. That was what people called the nearly 10,000 mostly Jewish children who were brought to Britain to escape from the Nazis. Most of them never saw their parents again and were the only members of their families to survive Hitler's mass killing of Jewish people, which we now call the Holocaust.

One of the children who arrived in the UK with the Kindertransport was Alf Dubs, who became a Member of Parliament and now has a seat in the House of Lords. Baron Dubs, as he is now called, has tried to help children who are arriving in the UK today without their parents. Many of them are fleeing from war in Syria, Iraq and Afghanistan. Baron Dubs campaigns for these children, who are refugees just as he was, to be allowed to come to the UK.

Chapter 3
Faisal

The match on Saturday was the first time the new team had played together. Sam arrived ten minutes early. His dad had come to watch. Hasan and Faisal were already there. Hasan was talking to his older brother, who was about to play on the next pitch. Faisal was standing to one side but not saying anything. Sam waited for them to finish talking. He was tying up his boots when Jordan arrived.

"I didn't think they would turn up," Jordan said, his voice a kind of grunt.

"Why wouldn't they?" Sam asked.

"They don't belong, do they?" Jordan said. "They've got a team of their own. Why do they want to take ours over?"

Sam didn't understand why Jordan didn't want two really good footballers in the team. "They're not trying to take over," he said. "They want to play football with kids their own age. They're joining our team. What's wrong with that?"

Jordan gave a shrug and walked away to talk to some of the other boys.

"He's a real charmer, isn't he?" Sam's dad said.

Sam shook his head. "He's always like that."

Hasan and Faisal came over, and Jack Rigby gave his team talk.

"OK, boys," he said. "We have had the same problem all season. We play the ball out of defence OK, but it's too slow. Our attacks just fall apart in the final third." He looked at the two new players. "Hasan and Faisal have got pace. They can help us turn things around."

"We need something," Kai said. "We're bottom of the table."

Jack nodded. "We're going to play Hasan in midfield, with Jordan and Faisal up top. We need you guys to play well together."

Faisal looked straight ahead. Jordan stared over at him. It was an angry stare.

*

The team Celtic was up against was called Five Ways. They were third from top. They kicked off and Celtic were pushed back straight away. Sam made two goal-line clearances in the first few minutes. Five Ways hit the post, and it went for a goal kick.

"So much for the new tactics," Jordan said. "They're really working, aren't they?"

Sam was sick of his moaning. "Give them a chance, will you?"

Hasan brought the ball down on his chest and turned, doing a one-two with Faisal. He slowed the ball, then looked for a pass. Jordan

was in space, so he swept it out to him. Jordan was slow to react, and the ball ran out of play.

"You left it on purpose," Sam said.

"Don't be daft," Jordan said as he walked back. "It was a bad pass. You've got to pass it to my feet."

Hasan put his hands on his hips and stared at Sam. "Why didn't he run for it?" he asked.

Sam knew the answer. Jordan didn't want Jack's plan to succeed. Every time Hasan or Faisal tried to give the ball to Jordan, something went wrong. And Jordan always put the blame on them. It was no surprise when Five Ways made the most of Jordan's poor play. They scored twice in five minutes. Celtic were 2–0 down at half-time.

"We're getting overrun in midfield," Jordan told Jack. "Leave me up top and put him back in midfield."

He didn't even say Faisal's name.

"We've got a game plan," Jack said. "We're going to stick with it."

Jordan scowled. "Don't blame me if it all goes pear-shaped," he said.

Nothing much changed in the second half. Hasan gave Jordan the ball. Sometimes Jordan lost it. Sometimes he kept it to himself instead of passing to Faisal. In the end, Hasan got fed up and decided to go it alone. He beat two players and powered into the Five Ways penalty area. At the last moment, he overran the ball, and a defender pushed it out for a corner. Hasan took the set-piece. Sam could see Jordan wasn't even trying to lose his marker. He wanted Hasan and Faisal gone, and this was his way of doing it.

Faisal had other ideas. As the ball came in, he ran into the area, climbed higher than anybody else and headed the ball home.

"Goal!"

The players mobbed Faisal. Celtic hadn't scored a goal like that for weeks. Even Jordan's mate Kai joined in. Jordan just stood to one side. Then he walked off on his own.

"Come on, boys," Jack shouted from the touchline. "We can win this."

Suddenly, it was all Celtic. Hasan and Faisal were at the heart of everything, but with five minutes to go, Celtic were still 2–1 down. Hasan picked up the ball in midfield. Jordan was running in space.

"Here. Here!" Jordan shouted.

At last, Jordan was finally trying. He saw a chance to score. Sam knew now that Jordan didn't play for the team, just for himself. He was a real glory-hunter. He just wanted to be the one to score the next goal.

"Pass it. Pass it!" Jordan yelled.

But Hasan had other ideas. He put his foot on the ball, turned and saw Faisal coming in from the left. He rolled the ball forward, and Faisal hit it on the volley. He smacked it into the net and peeled away, arms out wide like wings. Even then, he didn't say a word, but for once he was smiling.

Celtic had scored, but Jordan was angry. "That was a fluke," he said. "I had the best chance."

Sam shook his head. "Stop moaning," he said. "We got a draw. That's a point on the board, and it's no thanks to you."

Sam caught up with Hasan and Faisal.

Jordan had never been a friend. Now Sam had made him an enemy.

FRIENDSHIP THROUGH FOOTBALL

Refugees and asylum seekers are trying to escape from war and get to safety. When they arrive in the UK, they often have very little money and some of them don't speak English. They don't get to choose where they live and sometimes have to move around a lot. Sometimes, they have to leave Britain and are sent back to where they came from. It can be a very lonely and scary life.

Activities like sport can help refugees to settle in to their new home, have something to do and meet people. Sport helps people stay in good health, and that helps them to feel better about themselves.

Footballing clubs in the UK can help refugees become part of their local communities. For example, the City of Liverpool FC run a programme called Football for Everyone. They have helped over 300 refugees and asylum seekers. They give them equipment, coaching and kit. This helps refugees and asylum seekers feel less lonely. They can meet and play with local people. You don't need to speak English in order to kick a ball about with someone.

Everton in the Community also works with refugees. When former Everton manager Roberto Martinez came down to play football with the refugees, he said: "What it shows you is how powerful football can be when used in the right way." Smiling at someone else is easy, he explained. And just a smile can make a big difference to someone who is lonely and afraid.

Amnesty International, a group which tries to help refugees around the world, also believes that football is a great way to help people come together. They organised a weekend they called "Football Welcomes". It was a celebration of all that refugees in Britain have given to professional football since the Second World War. More than half of the clubs in the Premier League took part. Some put on special matches or gave away tickets, others set up tours of their stadiums or arranged visits from star players. This was their way of saying loud and clear that refugees are welcome in the UK.

Chapter 4
Missing

Sam was the second player to arrive for the next game, against Yew Tree Juniors. Kai had got there first.

"You look happy," Kai said.

Sam nodded.

"It's ages since we played as well as we did last Sunday," he said. "We could have won that match." He laughed. "We're not used to winning."

Kai looked awkward. "I know what you're thinking," he said. "Jordan's the one to blame for us only getting a draw."

"Look," Sam said, "I know he's your mate, but he's got to give Hasan and Faisal a chance. They're the best players we've got."

Kai looked around to make sure nobody else was there. He didn't want anyone to hear what he had to say. "I tried to say something to Jordan," he whispered, "but he won't listen."

Some of the other boys were making their way across the grass, so Kai didn't say anything else. Hasan was one of the last to arrive.

"Is Faisal here?" he asked.

"No," Sam said. "Why?"

"He was going to meet me at the gates, but he wasn't there. I don't get it."

"Are you worried?" Sam asked.

"A bit," Hasan said. "He has never been late before. He loves football."

Jack Rigby was about to give his team talk. "Where's Faisal?" he asked.

Hasan explained.

"Well, we can't wait much longer," Jack said. "We've got a game to play."

He waited for Faisal for a few more minutes, then got the boys together.

"OK," he said. "There's no sign of Faisal, so we'll have to play with Jordan on his own up front and an extra man in midfield. If Faisal turns up, I can bring him on as a sub. We've got two games to go in the season. One team goes down into the second division. That point last week moved us off the bottom. If we win both games, we stay up. We'll move the ball quickly and try to put Jordan in a good position to score."

The only player who looked happy was Jordan.

*

Yew Tree were two places above Celtic in the league, and it was even in the first twenty minutes. Neither side was ahead. Suddenly, Hasan lost his marker, sprinted down the wing and crossed the ball. Jordan had the goal at his mercy.

"Go on," Sam hissed. "Keep it low."

But Jordan leaned back and skied the ball over the bar. He turned, holding his head.

"It got a bobble," Jordan said.

Kai shook his head. "He's the bobble."

Everybody laughed. Just before half-time,
something happened to wipe the smiles from
their faces. Kai missed his pass, and Yew Tree
had two players closing in on the Celtic goal.
Yew Tree passed the ball between them, and
Sam watched the ball roll into the net. There
was nothing anyone could do about it.

"That's a sucker punch," he groaned.

Jack got the boys together. "Don't let your heads go down," he said. "You were the better team in the first half."

He was about to say something else when Faisal arrived. His jacket was covered in dirt and he had a mark on his face. Hasan took him to one side.

"I knew something had happened," Hasan said when they joined the others. "There's a group of teenagers that hang around and wait for Faisal. This time they threw things at him and chased him. One of them punched him in the face."

"That's disgusting," Kai said, and the other boys agreed.

The only one who didn't say a word was Jordan.

"Are you OK to play?" Jack asked.

Faisal nodded.

"You're playing up front on your own," Jack said. "Jordan, you're coming off."

"You're subbing me!" Jordan cried. "You can't do that. I'm the best player."

"You think you are," Sam said.

Jordan went for him, but Jack stepped between them.

"Knock it off," Jack said. "We won't have any fighting. You've had your worst game, Jordan. I've got to make changes."

Jordan stormed off and sat by himself away from everybody else.

"Spoiled brat," Kai said.

Sam grinned.

*

Faisal made the difference at the start of the second half. He was faster and stronger than Jordan, and he made himself a target for Hasan and the other boys. He came close twice, then Sam noticed Hasan swapping wings. Sam slipped the ball through, and Hasan put on a burst of speed. He jinked this way and that, then slotted the ball through to the waiting Faisal.

1–1.

Now it was all Celtic. Yew Tree did their best, but the ball kept coming back at them. Something had to give ... and it did. Celtic got three corners on the run. The third time Hasan swung it in, Faisal did an overhead kick, sweeping the ball into the roof of the net.

2–1 to Celtic.

Faisal got his hat-trick with a penalty. 3–1.

With two minutes to go, Faisal turned
provider. He went on a run. Now that Yew Tree
were playing deep and trying to stop Celtic
getting any more goals, Sam came forward.
Faisal saw him racing down the field and
rolled the ball to him. Sam ran onto the ball
and hammered it through into the goal. The
team celebrated as if they had just won the
Champions League. Jordan didn't join in. He
walked away with his head down.

"Ignore him," Kai said. "He'll get over it."

Sam turned to Faisal. "Are you OK walking
home by yourself?"

Faisal didn't answer, so Sam made him an
offer. "It isn't far out of my way," he said. "Why
don't a few of us go together?"

Faisal didn't live far. Hasan, Sam, Kai and
two other boys went with him. At the street
corner, they saw three teenagers.

"What's this?" one of them said. "Are you his bodyguards?"

Sam had an answer. "We're his mates. Leave him alone."

One of the teenagers shook his head. "It was only a bit of a laugh," he said.

"Hitting somebody isn't a bit of a laugh," Kai said.

The teenagers started walking away. "Suit yourselves," one of them said. "We've got better things to do than talk to a bunch of kids."

Faisal watched them go, but it was Hasan who spoke. "Thanks for coming with us," he said. "It makes a difference."

"No worries," Sam said. "We're a team."

REFUGEES AND FOOTBALL

Some refugees have become top footballers.

Saido Berahino, now a Stoke City player, made his name at West Bromwich Albion. Saido is a quick, skilful forward. He was born in Burundi in East Africa. His father died in the Burundian civil war. Saido travelled to England on his own at just ten years old. His mum and siblings had already left Burundi before him to escape the fighting, and he met up with them again in the UK.

Fabrice Muamba grew up in the Congo. When Fabrice was very young, his father had to flee the country because his life was in danger. Fabrice's father found safety in Britain, but it was three years before his family were able to join him. Fabrice was eleven years old when he arrived in the UK, and he found it very cold. He said, "It was the first time I had seen snow. I was shivering when I got off the plane, but it was worth it. We saw my father and we all ran up to each other and started hugging. It was the start of our new life."

Fabrice had a big scare in 2012 when he had a heart attack during a match between Bolton Wanderers and Spurs. His heart stopped beating for over 70 minutes, but he didn't die. He had to retire from football after his heart attack, and so he went to university to study sports journalism. Fabrice has had to deal with many problems in his life, but he has stayed strong.

Shefki Kuqi was a striker for teams including Sheffield Wednesday, Ipswich Town, Crystal Palace and Newcastle United. He had to flee from a terrible war in Kosovo when he was twelve. He moved to Finland with his family. He said that when they had to leave Kosovo, "Everybody was feeling sad and crying – it was like being at a funeral. I didn't really understand what was happening; all I knew was that I had to leave my home and all my friends."

Shefki played for his new country Finland 62 times. He had a special way of celebrating when he scored a goal. He would pretend to glide like a bird and then crash to the ground in a belly flop. The move led to him being called the "Flying Finn".

Chapter 5
Five words

Jordan didn't get over being taken off in the last match against Yew Tree. Jack Rigby had something to say to the team before the last game of the season. It was against Riverside United.

"There is no Jordan today," Jack told them. "His dad phoned me. He's quit the team."

Sam saw Hasan looking at him.

"It's no surprise, is it?" Sam said. "Jordan never wanted you and Faisal to join."

Hasan pulled a face. Faisal didn't seem to hear.

"We'll have to win without Jordan," Jack said.

"So who's going to be captain?" Sam asked.

Jack grinned. "You."

It wasn't going to be easy to beat Riverside. They were already champions and the best team in the league. Not only that. If Celtic lost, they might be going down into the lower division.

"How many games have we won all season?" Hasan asked.

"Two," Sam said, "and a few draws. That's why we're second from bottom. White Star are the bottom team, a point behind us. If we win today, we stay up. Any other result, we might be going down."

Hasan nodded.

"The good news," Sam said, "is that White Star are playing on the next pitch. We will know their score while we're playing."

Just as Sam was about to run onto the pitch ready for kick-off, Hasan tugged his sleeve. "Faisal said thanks for helping with those bullies," he whispered. "You and your mates were great. But he's had worse."

"Back home, you mean?" Sam said.

Hasan nodded. "Soldiers came to arrest his dad. He never saw him again. Then his mum died. That's why he's alone."

Sam listened. *How would it feel to have something like that happen?* Sam couldn't imagine it. "Does he have nightmares?" he asked.

Hasan nodded. "All the time."

*

Riverside attacked right from the kick-off. Their front players were strong and fast. Sam got in a couple of last-minute blocks and tackles, but it felt as if the attacks never stopped coming. Hasan and Faisal had to drop back to defend. It was like trying to dam a river.

"This is no good," Kai panted after they'd got through yet another attack. "Every time we boot it down field, they come right back at us. We are being overrun."

"Yes," Sam said, "but we need everybody in defence at the moment."

In the end, it all got too much. Another cross came in, low and hard, from the wing. It caused panic in Celtic's defence. Kai tried to clear it, but he hit the ball against Sam's back. The ball spun off Sam and smacked into the roof

of the net. He heard somebody laugh behind
him. He knew who it was.

"Jordan," he grumbled. Jordan had turned up
to watch them play. "I thought he didn't want to
play any more."

"He doesn't," Kai said. "He wants to laugh at
us when we go down."

Sam looked over at Jordan. It was true. He
had just come to cause trouble.

Things got worse ten minutes later. The Riverside striker burst into the penalty area. The Celtic keeper tried to collect the ball but made contact and brought him down. It was a penalty.

2–0 down.

Just then, there was a big shout from the next pitch.

"Oh, bad luck, boys," Jordan said with a big grin. "White Star have just scored. You're going to get relegated."

Celtic had other ideas. They defended the best they could. After some scary moments, they got to half-time without conceding another goal to Riverside.

"This isn't working," Jack said. "We can't just defend. Look, we may as well lose 5–0 as 2–0. If we attack, we might just get something. Let's try it. Hasan and Faisal, stay up the pitch. We'll just have to hope our defence can keep Riverside out."

Riverside attacked from the kick-off, but Sam got in a tackle. He looked up and saw Hasan had lost his man. He was running into space and holding his arm up, calling for the ball. Sam hit his pass low and hard, and Hasan ran onto it. Faisal was moving this way and that, trying to find some space. Hasan flicked the ball to his left, and Faisal hit it sweetly into the net. The Riverside boys looked stunned. They weren't used to letting in goals, especially to losers like Celtic.

"Great pass," Hasan said. "We chose the right guy to be captain."

That made Sam feel proud, but his team was still 2–1 down. And on the next pitch, White Star were winning. Sam looked over at Jordan. Jordan held up three fingers with one hand and made a zero with his other hand. White Star were 3–0 up. Celtic had to win their match now.

"Come on, lads," Sam said. "We just need two goals. We can do it!"

Sam went ahead. He tackled, he put in blocks and he made passes. He was making all the other boys play better. Kai picked up the ball and dribbled through the Riverside defence, laying it off. Hason smashed the ball into the back of the net.

2–2.

"One more goal, lads," Sam cried. "One more and we've done it."

And it came. This time it was pure brilliance from Faisal. He picked up the ball on the halfway line, beat two players and chipped the keeper.

3–2.

Everybody was smiling. They'd done it. They were going to stay up.

"How long?" Sam called over to Jack.

Jack held up five fingers.

"Five minutes," Sam said. "Only five minutes to go. Keep it tight."

The seconds ticked away, and Riverside were all over the Celtic defence. To Sam's horror, the ball spun clear and ran between Kai and Hasan. In a stroke of bad luck, it fell right into the Riverside striker's path.

3–3.

Sam looked for Jack. "How long left?" he asked, unable to believe their bad luck.

"A minute," Jack told him. "White Star are still three up. It's all or nothing. A draw is no good to us. Go for it!"

Sam joined Hasan and Faisal in the centre circle. The ref was looking at his watch. Then something happened that made Sam's mouth fall open.

Faisal spoke. "Give me the ball."

Faisal dropped back, looking down the field.

"You can't score from your own half," Sam said.

Faisal stared at him. "Give me the ball."

Sam rolled it across. Faisal took a single step and hit it into the air. The Riverside keeper saw the danger and started to back-pedal. The ball was spinning towards him. It was as if time had stopped. The ball was dropping. Still, the keeper was running back. He flung his hands in the air, but the ball went through them ... and landed in the back of the net.

Then Faisal roared a single word. "Goal!"

The Celtic players all piled on top of Faisal, congratulating him.

"Let him up," Sam said at last. "We're going to crush him."

Faisal didn't care about being crushed. He was laughing.

After a bit, Riverside restarted the game, but the ref blew the whistle before they could make any progress. The Celtic players raised their arms. It was all over. They were going to stay up.

"Where's Jordan?" Sam asked.

"Gone," Kai told him. "He looked sick when Faisal's goal went in. He thought we were finished."

"Well, we showed him, didn't we?" Sam said.

He turned to Faisal. "So you're talking now?" he said.

Faisal just looked at him. Five words were all Sam was getting. There had been enough miracles for one day.

Our books are tested
for children and young people by
children and young people.

Thanks to everyone who consulted on
a manuscript for their time and effort in
helping us to make our books better
for our readers.

MORE GREAT FOOTBALL STORIES PACKED WITH FACTS

Alan Gibbons

DREAM TEAM

ISBN: 978-1-78112-771-1

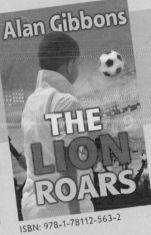

Alan Gibbons

THE LION ROARS

ISBN: 978-1-78112-563-2

Alan Gibbons

THE BEAUTIFUL GAME

ISBN: 978-1-78112-691-2

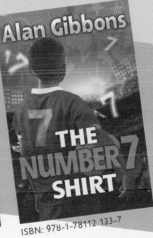

Alan Gibbons

THE NUMBER 7 SHIRT

ISBN: 978-1-78112-133-7